When I'm Feeling
Kind

Written and illustrated by Trace Moroney

The Five Mile Press

When I'm feeling kind
I feel soft and gentle and caring . . .
and my heart feels really warm.

When I'm feeling kind
I like to do things that help other people.

Feeling kind helps me understand
how other people may be feeling.

There are many things
that I like to do
when I feel kind . . .
like help Mum
clean the house . . .

or *listen*
to a friend
talk about
a problem
they have . . .

or give a friend a big hug
when they feel sad.

Kindness is something I can also
give to *myself.*

Being kind to myself means
liking who I am and being proud
of the things I'm good at . . .

instead of worrying about the things
I'm not so good at!

Being kind to myself means
looking after my body.
I look after it by eating healthy food,

exerci

day and getting lots of sleep!

When I'm feeling kind
I find it easy to be polite and have good manners.
When I ask for something
I always say . . .

please

and when someone gives me something
I always say . . .

thank you

Kindness is something that makes
everyone feel really good . . .
especially me!

Background Notes for Parents

Self-esteem is the key

The greatest gift you can give your child is healthy self-esteem. Children who *feel valuable,* and who *trust themselves* have positive self-esteem. You can help your child *feel valuable* by spending quality time with him or her, playing games, reading books, or just listening. You can also help children *feel valuable* by helping them discover and become the person they want to be. Success follows people who genuinely *like who they are.*

However, happiness is more than just being successful. Helping your child gain the self-trust needed to deal with failure, loss, shame, difficulty and defeat is as important – if not more so – than succeeding or being best. When children trust themselves to handle painful feelings – fear, anger and sadness – they gain an *inner* security that allows them to embrace the world in which they live.

Each of these *FEELINGS* books has been carefully designed to help children better understand their feelings, and in doing so, gain greater autonomy (freedom) over their lives. Talking about feelings teaches children that it is normal to feel sad, or angry, or scared at times. With greater tolerance of painful feelings, children become free to enjoy their world, to feel secure in their abilities, and to be happy.

Feeling KIND

Kindness flows naturally from a child with a healthy self-esteem. Kindness is like sunshine because it makes everybody feel warm and cared about. Kindness is sharing our caring and good feelings with others – especially with those feeling sad or lonely. There are endless opportunities to teach your children about kindness in your everyday activities. If children are treated with kindness, they will value themselves and want to extend kindness to others – including animals. Most importantly, when children act in kind ways they not only like who they are, they also create a better world for those they meet along the way.

Written by psychologists Bill Hallam and Dr Craig Olsson

For Emma and Samuel

The Five Mile Press Pty Ltd
1 Centre Road, Scoresby
Victoria 3179 Australia
www.fivemile.com.au

First published 2006

National Library of Australia Cataloguing-in-Publication data
Moroney, Trace
When I'm feeling kind.

For children
ISBN 978 1 74178 115 1 (hardback)

I. Title.

A823.3

Printed in China 10 9

Visit Trace Moroney at www.tracemoroney.com